آگوستوس و لبخندش

Augustus and his Smile

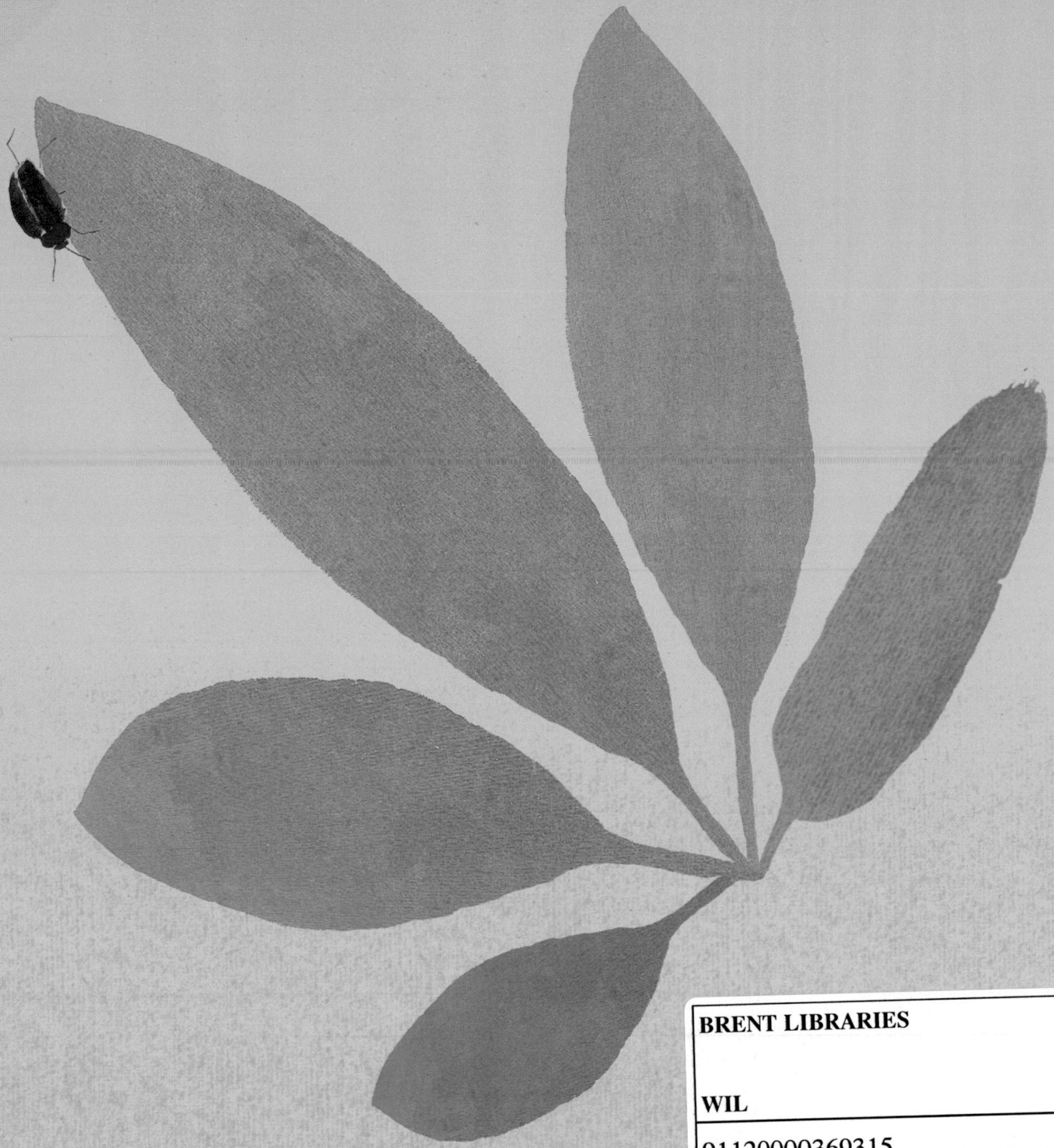

آگوستوس و لبخندش

Augustus and his Smile

Catherine Rayner

Farsi translation by
Anwar Soltani

آگوستوس ببره، غمگین بود.
او لبخندش را گم کرده بود.

Augustus the tiger was sad.
He had lost his smile.

بنابراین هیکلش را محکم و ببرانه کشید و به راه افتاد تا پیدایش کند.

So he did a HUGE tigery stretch and set off to find it.

اول، زیر انبوهی از بوته‌ها خزید. آنجا سوسک کوچک برّاقی دید، اما لبخندش را نتوانست پیدا کند.

First he crept under a cluster of bushes. He found a small, shiny beetle, but he couldn't see his smile.

Then he climbed to the tops of the tallest trees.
He found birds that chirped and called,
but he couldn't find his smile.

بعد، تا نوک بلندترین درختها بالا رفت.

پرنده‌ها را دید که جیک جیک میکردند و میخواندند،

اما لبخندنش را نتوانست پیدا کند.

آگوستوس بیشتر و بیشتر گشت.

تا قلّهٔ بلندترین کوهها بالا رفت، جائی که
ابرهای برفی میچرخیدند، و در هوای
یخبندان طرحهای یخی میساختند.

Further and further Augustus searched.
He scaled the crests of the highest mountains where the
snow clouds swirled, making frost patterns in the freezing air.

او تا ته گودترین اقیانوسها شنا کرد و با گلّه‌ای از ماهیهای کوچک براق شلپ و شلوپ راه انداخت.

He swam to the bottom of the deepest oceans and splished and splashed with shoals of tiny, shiny fish.

در میان پهناورترین دشتها بالا و پائین رفت، و در زیر آفتاب شکلهای سایه‌ای ساخت. آگوستوس از میان شنهای رونده جلو و جلوتر رفت.

تا اینکه ...

He pranced and paraded through
the largest desert, making
shadow shapes in the sun.
Augustus padded further
    and further
        through shifting sand
            until ...

... pitter patter

pitter patter

drip

drop

plop!

... شُر شُر

شُر شُر

چِک

چِک

تالاپ!

همانطور که دانه‌های باران می‌جهیدند

و جاری می‌شدند،

آگوستوس هم رقصید

و دوید.

Augustus danced
and raced
as raindrops bounced
and flew.

شلپ و شلوپ کنان از میان بِرکه‌ها گذشت، بِرکه‌هائی بزرگتر و گودتر

به سوی بِرکه‌ای بزرگ و نقره‌ای – آبی دوید و دید ...

He splashed through puddles, bigger and deeper.
He raced towards a huge silver-blue puddle
and saw ...

... لبخندش
... آنجا زیر دماغش است!

... there under his nose
... his smile!

و آگوستوس فهمید هرگاه خوشحال باشد، لبخندش هم با او خواهد بود.

او پیشتر، تنها میبایست با ماهیها شنا کند یا در بِرکه‌ها

برقصد، یا از کوهها بالا برود و دنیا را

بپاید — تا شادی ای را که همه جا دور و بر او بود بیابد.

آگوستوس چنان خوشحال بود که لی لی کرد و

به ورجه ورجه افتاد ...

And Augustus realised that his smile would be there, whenever he was happy.

He only had to swim with the fish or dance in the puddles, or climb the mountains and look at the world – for happiness was everywhere around him.

Augustus was so pleased that
he hopped
and skipped …

... و لبخندزنان از جایش پرید.

... and jumped away,
smiling.

Amazing tiger facts

Augustus is a Siberian tiger.

Siberian tigers are the biggest cats in the world!
They live in Southern Russia and Northern China
where the winters are very cold.

Most tigers are orange with black stripes.
The stripes make them hard to see when they
walk through tall weeds and grasses.

Tigers are good swimmers and like to cool down
by sitting in waterholes.

Each tiger's stripes are different to those of
other tigers – like a human finger print.

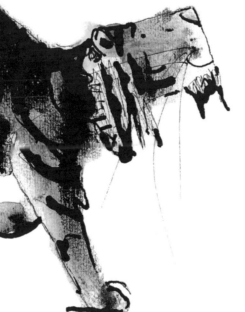

Tigers are in danger ...

Tigers are only hunted by one animal ... HUMANS!
And humans are ruining the land on which tigers live.

There are more tigers living in zoos and nature reserves than
in the wild. There are only about 6000 tigers left in the wild.

Help save the tiger!

World Wildlife Fund (WWF)
Panda House
Weyside Park
Godalming
Surrey GU7 1XR
Tel: 01483 426 444
www.wwf.org.uk

David Shepherd Wildlife
Foundation
61 Smithbrook Kilns
Cranleigh
Surrey GU76 8JJ
Tel: 01483 727 323/267 924
www.davidshepherd.org